9.95

FEB 21 2006

EAST MEADOW PUBLIC LIBRARY

3 1299 00735 3338

P9-CBB-452

This book belongs to:

J EASY A

PARENTING

✓

EAST MEADOW PUBLIC LIBRARY
1886 FRONT STREET
EAST MEADOW, NY 11554
(516) 794 – 2570

5 × 3/13

BAKER & TAYLOR

MARTHA ALEXANDER

Nobody Asked ME
If I Wanted a Baby Sister

ini Charlesbridge

Text copyright © 1971 by Martha Alexander
Illustrations copyright © 2006 by Martha Alexander
All rights reserved, including the right of reproduction in whole or in part in any form.
Charlesbridge and colophon are registered trademarks of Charlesbridge Publishing, Inc.

Published by Charlesbridge
85 Main Street
Watertown, MA 02472
(617) 926-0329
www.charlesbridge.com

Library of Congress Cataloging-in-Publication Data
Alexander, Martha G.
Nobody asked me if I wanted a baby sister / Martha Alexander.
p. cm.
Summary: Resenting the attention and praise lavished on his new baby
sister, Oliver tries to give her away to several people in the neighborhood.
ISBN-13: 978-1-57091-679-3; ISBN-10: 1-57091-679-9 (reinforced for library use)
[1. Brothers and sisters—Fiction.] I. Title.
PZ7.A3777   No 2006
[E]—dc22
2005009912

Printed in China
(hc) 10 9 8 7 6 5 4 3 2 1

Illustrations recolorized with watercolor and colored pencil
on the pages of a first-edition printing of the original book
Display type and text type set in Roger and New Aster
Color separations by Chroma Graphics, Singapore
Printed and bound by Jade Productions
Production supervision by Brian G. Walker
Designed by Diane M. Earley

For Kimi and her brood—Lisa, Christina, Leslie, and Beau
—M. A.

"Oh, Mrs. Applebaum, what a beautiful baby!"
"How chubby she is!"
"What pretty blue eyes she has!"

"Hi, Amy, Alice, and Phyllis! Would your
mother like to have a beautiful baby?"

"Sure, if it's a boy."

"Mister, would you like a beautiful, chubby baby?"

"Well, sonny, maybe we could use her in our act. Can she balance a ball?"

"Say, folks, would you like this beautiful, chubby, blue-eyed baby? That basket would be perfect for her to ride in."

"I never thought of that. But we're going
to have our own baby soon! Thanks anyway!"

"I give up. Nobody wants you."

"Hey, Toby, do you know anybody who wants
a baby that nobody wants?"

"Sure, my mom. She loves babies."

"Look what we brought you, Mom!"
"Oh, what a nice baby!

What's the matter, baby? Are you hungry?

Not hungry? Do you need a diaper change?

No, her diaper's fine. Maybe she just
doesn't like me. You take her, Jane."

"This baby's impossible!
Ouch! She's pulling my hair!"

"What a loud-mouth baby!"

"Be quiet, loud-mouth baby!"

"Why, Oliver, it's *you* she wants!"

"You know, Bonnie, you're a lot smarter
than I thought. Let's go tell Mom.

When you get big enough, maybe we could
play horse and wagon."